For Captain Nemo

First published in the United States 2002 by
Dial Books for Young Readers
A division of Penguin Putnam Inc.
345 Hudson Street
New York, New York 10014
Published in Great Britain 2001 by Jonathan Cape
The Random House Group Limited
Copyright © 2001 by Babette Cole
Printed in Singapore

1 3 5 7 9 10 8 6 4 2

Library of Congress Cataloging-in-Publication Data
Cole, Babette.
Truelove / Babette Cole.
p.   cm.
Summary: When a new baby arrives, Truelove the puppy must teach
his family that there is enough love to go around.
ISBN 0-8037-2717-8
[1. Dogs—Fiction. 2. Babies—Fiction. 3. Love—Fiction.]
I. Title: True Love. II. Title.
PZ7.C6734 Tt 2002
[E]—dc21   2001028022

TRUELOVE

Babette Cole

Dial Books for Young Readers New York

"Now that they have a new baby,
will there be enough love for both of us?"

Love feels like a warm puppy.

"OW!"

Love means sharing.

"*Truelove, no!*"

Love cures all hurt.

"Oh, well."

Love gives you strength.